THE MIDNIGHT SCRIBE

a Mary MacIntosh Novel

Maureen Anne Meehan

THE MIDNIGHT SCRIBE

Copyright © 2024 by Maureen Anne Meehan

ISBN: 979-8-3304-8122-4 (e)

www. maureenmeehanbooks.com

info@maureenmeehan.com

Table of Contents

AUTHOR'S NOTE

In this novel, I attempt to delve into the struggles of mothers who work and raise their children and support their families. Decisions are difficult, and women are judged for these decisions and it is unfair.

Women are kind, loving and hard-working and will defend their young to the death. Watch Mother Nature. Grizzly 399 in Yellowstone National Park died this year at age 28. She was the mother of at least 18 cubs, and she was the best grizzly mom in the park. Pray that her one-year-old cub survives the winter on his or her own without a momma bear.

Growing up in Wyoming, we fall in love with our wildlife. This novel has little to do with wildlife, but 399 is also dedicated to this amazing grizzly.

DEDICATION

The Midnight Scribe is dedicated to all victims of violent crime. These tragedies affect millions of people worldwide, and they are unacceptable. Women are most at risk of being victims of violent crime, shy of gang-related harm.

Women tend to serve in loving and supportive roles, and this makes us vulnerable, unfortunately. I have been a victim of attempted rape, and it scars me for life. I use my literally talent for retribution to these perpetrators, and it is better than therapy.

Survivors and thrives inspire us all, as we have a choice every day when we awake with the blessing of a new day. We are allowed to choose positivity and strength.

This novel is dedicated to all victims and their respective support groups of violent crime—Godspeed in healing.

Chapter 1

Edgar Allan Poe (1809-1848) was a legendary American writer, poet, editor, and literary critic, known for his macabre and gothic works that shaped modern horror, mystery, and detective fiction. Born January 19, 1908, in Boston into parents who were traveling actors. His father, David Poe, Jr., abandoned the family, and his mother, Elizam died of tuberculosis when he was three years old. He was welcomed by John and Frances Allan of Richmond, Virginia, though they never formally adopted him. They provided him with a good education, but had a tumultuous relationship, mostly due to financial disagreement.

Poe attended the University of Virginia in 1826 but had to leave due to gambling debts and lack of support from his pseudo-father figure, John Allen. He briefly enrolled at the United States Military Academy at West Point but was expelled after deliberately neglecting duties.

Poe began his literary career as a poet and published his first book, Tamerlane and Other Poems, in 1827. He worked as an editor for several literary magazines, gaining a reputation for sharp literary criticism.

His breakthrough came with the 1841 publication of "The Murders in the Rue Morgue," considered by many as the first modern detective story. "The Raven" in 1845 brought him national fame, though not financial stability.

Poe often explored themes of mortality, the macabre, and the fragility of life. Many of his works delve into the dark recesses of the human mind, exploring guilt, madness, and fear.

Poetry for him must have been fascinating with a concentration on love, loss, and idealized visions perhaps of his mother and her beauty. He felt a sense of abandonment, but he was reconciled with her natural death. He likely despised his father for walking out on the family.

Ghosts, spirits, and eerie phenomena remained central to many of his stories, and remain forefront in the memories of artists.

His literary works that did assist in his fame and fortune include "The Tell-Tale Heart" (1843) which is a chilling exploration of guilt and madness. "The Fall of the Household Usher" (1839) is a gothic tale of decay and supernatural terror. "The Cask of Amontillado" (1846) is a tale of dark and evil revenge. "The Masque of the Red Death" (1842) is a symbolic tale about the inevitability of death.

His poetry describes him deeply, including "The Raven" (1845) which he remains most famous for, reflecting themes of grief and longing, likely regarding his mother.

"Annabel Lee" (1849) is a lyrical exploration of eternal love, again, likely his feelings of missing his mom. "Lenore" (1843) is a lament of a lost lover, and "The Bells" (1849) is a romantic and onomatopoeic masterpiece.

Edgar Allan Poe was also an excellent criminologist in the sense that he crafted detective fiction prior to a time when it was a savvy notion. "The Murders in the Rue Morgue" (1841) introduced C. Auguste Dupin as his prototype for modern fictional detectives such as Sherlock Holmes. "The Purlointed Letter" (1844) is another Dupin masterpiece showcasing Poe's ingenuity in plot design.

Poe married his 13-year-old cousin, Virginia Clemn, in 1836, and she remained a source of inspiration but suffered from ill health and also died of tuberculosis, like his mother. These losses deeply darkened him. He struggled with poverty, alcoholism, and mental health issues.

Edgar Allan Poe died mysteriously on October 7, 1849, in Baltimore at the age of 40 and the cause of death remains unknown, with theories ranging from alcoholism, rabies, and cholera, but the most popular cause of death for him, based on his life was a form of revenge concerning his fraudulent misgivings with finances. He was found delirious on the streets of Baltimore, wearing clothes that were not his own, and his last words were reportedly, "Lord, help my poor soul."

The note pinned to the first victim of the Midnight Scribe serial killer mirrored the note of Edgar Allan Poe. This middle-aged man who was found dead on a street corner on the streets of Baltimore, had the inscription that said, "Lord, help my poor soul," and the handwriting could be described as that of the famous author, Edgar Allan Poe.

Chapter 2

Baltimore, Maryland, 2024, November 23, Charles Street. A National Scenic Byway that connects the city's historic and cultural attractions with the suburbs of Baltimore, was the scene of a brutal crime.

The Midnight Scribe murdered a victim while emulating Edgar Allan Poe in an area home to world-class attractions and museums, including the Homewood House Museum, the Lacrosse Museum and the National Hall of Fame. This thoroughfare in North America leads to downtown Baltimore and the Inner Harbor, which has many attractions, including the Maryland Science Center, National Aquarium, Port Discovery, and The Children's Museum. Other notables include Fells Point Main Street featuring a mix of locally owned shops, restaurants, bars, hotels, art galleries, and small businesses, as well as Cathedral Street, a major north-south Avenue in Mount Vernon, named for the National Shrine of the Assumption.

East Lombard Street includes "corned beef row," which was once the center of Jewish life in Baltimore.

Charles Street, near the harbor, port and aquarium, was where the Midnight Scribe murdered his first victim. The victim remained a John Doe, as he was likely a homeless drug addict, and he was found stabbed to death in a brutal attack, and had a note pinned to his chest that read, in handwriting similar to that of Edgar Allan Poe, that read "Lord, help my poor soul."

Chapter 3

Jack the Ripper is one of the most infamous and enigmatic serial killers in history and he terrified the streets of London for years. His identity remains a mystery, and his crimes have inspired countless books, movies, and theories. He is believed to have murdered at least five women in the Whitechapel district of London in 1888. These victims, known as the "canonical five," were all prostitutes.

Mary Ann Nichols was murdered on August 31. 1888. Annie Chapman was killed on September 8, 1888. Elizabeth Stride died at his hands-on September 30, 1888, and on that same night, he killed Catherine Eddowes. Mary Jane Kelly was killed on November 9, 1888.

The killings were marked by extreme brutality, with mutilation of the victims' bodies. The level of precision led some to speculate that the killer had medical or anatomical knowledge.

Several factors combined to Jack the Ripper's enduring infamy. The name "Jack the Ripper" came from a letter sent to the police, allegedly by the killer, though its authenticity is debated. Despite extensive investigations, the police never identified the killer.

Over 100 suspects have been proposed, including Montague John Druitt, who was a barrister with a long history of mental illness.   Druitt was not only a barrister but also a teacher from a well-off family.   He drowned himself in the River Thames shortly after the final canonical order. Some believe his death ended the killings.

Aaron Kosminski was a Polish barber who had sharp instruments, cut hair and shaved men with great precision. Identified by a witness as the killer, he was investigated thoroughly, but the witness refused to testify in court.   DNA from a scarf linked to one of the victims has been controversially connected to Kosminski, but the DNA evidence was widely disputed due to contamination and poor documentation.

Walter Sickert was an artist.   Patricia Cornwell's theory suggested that he left clues in his artwork and had an obsession with the murders. However, no solid evidence tied him to the crimes, and many historians dismiss Cornwell's claims as speculative.

Prince Albert Victor was a member of the royal family as he was Queen Victoria's grandson.   The prince's alleged connections to prostitutes and supposed mental instability have fueled conspiracy theories. However, he had alibis for most of the murders, and the theory is largely seen as sensationalism.

Dr. Francis Tumblety was an American whack doctor and was arrested in London around the time of the murders for unrelated charges. Known for misogynistic views and owning a collection of uteruses made him fit the crimes, but there was no direct line to Whitechapel or the victims.

Some theories suggest that Jack the Ripper may have been a woman, or that the murders were the work of multiple people. The canonical five murders were committed plausibly by one lone killer with surgical knowledge, possibly a local with intimate knowledge of Whitechapel's street.

Another theory suggests the murders were ritualistic or part of a cover-up involving high-ranking officials or royals tied to the Freemasons. This idea was popularized in From Hell.

Some people believe that the killer was a woman called "Jill the Ripper" a midwife or a woman disguised as a man. This theory argues that a midwife could explain surgical precision.

Some believe that there were multiple killers. Most agree that Victorian-era policing faced significant challenges such as a lack of forensic science, as no fingerprinting, DNA analysis, or advanced tools existed at the time. In addition, the Metropolitan Police and the City of London Police operated independently, leading to jurisdictional disputes and delayed sharing of evidence.

Hundreds of false leads, hoax letters, and sensationalist media coverage misdirected investigators, as there was an overwhelming sense of public hysteria.

Class bias focused investigations on lower-class immigrants such as Jews and Eastern Europeans, potentially overlooking wealthy suspects. The area where the murders took place was known for extreme poverty, overcrowded slums, homelessness, and poor sanitation characterized as conditions of East End London at the time. Prostitution was a problem as well, as many women turned to tricks to survive poverty. The victims lived precarious lives on the margins of society. to this an influx of Jewish immigrants from Eastern Europe which created racial and cultural tensions, leading to scapegoating. Gender inequality was a factor as well, as women were often viewed as property or moral failures, making them vulnerable targets. The press sensationalized the murders, coining the term "Jack the Ripper." Newspapers like The Star competed to publish lurid details, amplifying public fear and fascination.

The Ripper case has fascinated historians, criminologists, and writers for over a century. It has been the inspiration for the books, From Hell by Alan Moore, and Portrait of a Killer by Patricia Cornwell.

It was the basis of the film, From Hell in 2001, and Jack the Ripper in 1959.

Tied to Freemasonry, the royal family, and secret societies, Jack the Ripper has been the subject of many conspiracy theories. The case is a fascinating mix of real horror, investigative failures, and social turmoil.

Over 100 suspects have been proposed, but few stand out due to circumstantial evidence or intriguing connections.

Linking Jack the Ripper to the Midnight Scribe Killer included calling cards of handwritten letters in Victorian-era cursive, mockery of police, historical cosplay in that this second victim had been re-dressed in period-appropriate attire, and the cipher note.

The second victim of the Midnight Scribe Killer had a short letter written in blood in the victim's hand. The note contained a cipher inspired by Jack the Ripper's taunting style, which needed solving to understand the killer's motive and next move. The cipher was uncoded to read, "When the moon is crescent, the fifth star shall fall." This victim also had surgical cuts and gruesome mutilation but with deliberate symbolism in the form of a cryptic phrase and the date of death carved into the victim's abdomen. Also, there was a carving of a miniature gaslight lamp.

John Douglas, the FBI criminal profiler believed that the Midnight Scribe Killer had a deep connection between his murders and that of Jack the Ripper. It linked unsolved cases, correcting the Ripper's "mistakes" and a continuation of what John believed could be a serial killer with a motive.

The note left behind was very problematic because it accused Mary MacIntosh of being part of a lineage of "keepers of secrets" tied to Jack the Ripper, which is why John called Mac to tell her about the serial killings in Florida and to invite her to help him and the FBI with the case.

Chapter 4

"I need your help, Mac," John Douglas said to Mac. "We have two murders now by the Midnight Scribe, and the ciphers and letters he leaves behind are getting more specific and serious."

"Hi, John. Nice to hear from you," Mac started. "I read the file on the first murder. When did the second one happen?"

"Two nights ago. It made national news I am surprised that you haven't heard," John said. "But I know that you have your hands full with the birth of your twin girls last month, and the twin boys that are, what, about 18 months old by now," John continued.

"I don't have time to shower, let alone read a newspaper or watch television," Mac said. "All I do is run around after the boys with at least one infant in my arms. It's massive chaos here."

"You need more help," he said. "Thank goodness you didn't seek reelection as city prosecutor."

"There is no way I could work full time anymore. Like I said, I barely have time to shower or eat," Mac said. "And

I have a part-time nanny, my mother-in-law's help, and Burg is a great support. It's just that we had four babies in 15 months. Good news, though. Burg got snipped, so no more babies."

"Thank goodness."

"He was such a baby about the procedure, with a bag of frozen peas on his privates and whining. I wanted to throat-punch him after giving birth to two sets of twins the old-fashioned way!"

"Getting back to the case, is there any way that you can consult with my team from the FBI? We have a weird dilemma with this most recent murder. I have emailed you the killer's cipher and letter left on the victim. This victim seems to have been dressed up like Jack the Ripper and the killer specifically mentions your name in the cipher. He accuses you of being part of the secret society within the Freemasons," John said.

"What!? That's ridiculous," Mac said. "That scares me a little, John. That means that this guy knows who I am."

"Everyone knows who you are after you solved the Dating Game killings, the Red Hand murders, the Deputy Dawg murder, and I could go on and on," John said. "You've been on the national news for years with these crimes."

"I suppose. Send me what you have and when I hopefully get all four of these kids down for a nap, I will take a peek at the file and summarize my thoughts," Mac agreed.

"Thank you! I was prepared for you to decline."

"Burg will think I'm crazy, but I am intrigued, especially in light of being mentioned specifically in this most recent murder," Mac said. "Can you please have the FBI team send me our engagement letter so that I get paid for this?"

"It's already in your inbox along with the file I just sent," John stated.

"Ok, thanks. I'll take a look as soon as the kiddos go down for their nap," Mac said before hanging up.

"Burg, I am forwarding you and email that John sent earlier. He is tracking a serial killer in Florida that they are calling 'The Midnight Scribe,' and this guy left a cipher on a note on the latest victim that mentions me by name. I'm worried.

I just called our handyman and asked him to install a security system at our house and he will arrive later this afternoon to do so," Mac said to her husband.

"What? The note mentions you by name? That is unnerving. Good call regarding the security system. We probably should have installed one when we bought the new house," Burg said.

"Agreed. The handyman is installing eight ring cameras on the perimeter and an alarm inside. It's not cheap," Mac warned.

"Safety first. I don't care about the cost. We need to protect our family."

Mac continued to purview the serial killer file, this time in more detail. The fact that the Midnight Scribe left ciphers that resembled the Zodiac Killer was concerning, and the idea that he staged the murder scene after the killing reminded her of the Dating Game Killer.

Chapter 5

Cleopatra VII Philopater *69 BCE – 30 BCE) was the last active ruler of the Ptolemaic Kingdom of Egypt, renowned for her intelligence, political acumen, and influence. As a member of the Macedonian Greek dynasty founded by Ptolemy I Soter, a general under Alexander the Great, Cleopatra reigned during a time of immense political upheaval.   Mac opened the file that John Douglas sent and started to read about the two murders recently in Dade County, Miami, and she was frightened by the cipher left in a note on the latest victim, called by the FBI, Jack the Ripper Squared.   Whoever this serial killer was, he was keenly aware of her work with the FBI on the recent murders in Wyoming. That could not bear well for her family's safety, and after reading the file cover to cover, she called her husband who was the local Sheriff in Sheridan.

She was born in 69 BCE in Alexandria and was the daughter of Ptolemy XII Auletes and possibly Cleopatra V Tryphaena.   She was highly educated, fluent in multiple languages (Egyptian, Greek, Latin, Hebrew, and others), and well-versed in philosophy, science, and literature.

Unlike her predecessors, she embraced Egyptian culture and was the first in her dynasty to learn the Egyptian language, positioning herself as a true Egyptian ruler. She initially co-ruled with her father and later with her brothers, Ptolemy XIII and Ptolemy XIV, as was customary under Ptolemaic law. After her father's death in 51 BCE, she became co-ruler with her brother, Ptolemy XIII. However, conflicts over power led to civil war.

Cleopatra famously aligned herself with Julius Caesar to secure her throne. She was smuggled into Caesar's palace, allegedly in a rolled-up carpet, to meet him, a move that showcased her resourcefulness and charisma. Their political and personal relationship resulted in a son, Ptolemy XV Philopator Philometor Caesar, commonly called Caesarion.

After Caesar's assassination in 44 BCE, Cleopatra aligned with Mark Antony, a member of the Roman triumvirate. Their union was both romantic and strategic, as Antony needed Cleopatra's wealth and military support for his campaigns, while she sought to secure her dynasty's survival. They had three children together: Alexander Helios, Cleopatra Selene II, and Ptolemy Philadelphia.

Cleopatra and Antony's relationship and their declaration of Caesarion as Ceasar's heir angered Octavian Augustus, Caesar's adopted son and heir. In 31 BCE, their forces were defeated by Octavan's navy at the Battle of Actium.

After Octavian captured the city of Alexandria, Mark Antony committed suicide, believing Cleopatra was dead. She died shortly thereafter, reportedly by the bite of an asp or cobra, though the exact cause remains debated.

Following her death, Egypt became a Roman province, ending the Ptolemaic dynasty.

Cleopatra is remembered as a complex figure: a ruler who wields immense political power and influence in a male-dominated world. Ancient Roman propaganda depicted her as a dangerous seductress who manipulated powerful men, but modern historians recognize her as a shrewd leader and diplomat. She has inspired countless works of art, literature, and film, remaining an enduring symbol of beauty, intelligence and ambition.

The Midnight Scribe chose Cleopatra as his next victim in an opulent and evocative Cleopatra grandeur. A modern recreation of an ancient Egyptian palace, complete with richly decorated pillars, flickering candlelight, and golden statues of deities like Isis and Horus was the scene of the murder.

The victim, dressed in s flowing white tunic and a striking headdress adorned with turquoise and lapis lazuli, was found lying dramatically on a low golden chaise. The scene was a depiction of Cleopatra's alleged death scene. Nearby, polished alabaster um contained a live cobra coiled ominously – a nod to the traditional story of Cleopatra's demise. Upon closer inspection, however, the victim did not die from a snakebite but from a meticulously inflicted wound at the base of the neck, designed to mimic the fang marks of an asp.

Scattered rose petals, honey-scented oils, and shattered perfume bottles filled the air with an intoxicating aroma, creating a macabre yet poetic atmosphere. The killer placed a replica of Cleopatra's signet ring on the victim's finger – a chilling signature detail.

On a piece of parchment, carefully aged to appear ancient, the killer left a letter written in hieroglyphics interspersed with cryptic English phrases. The hieroglyphs, when translated, formed part of a cipher revealing the killer's next target. The letter read: "She thought herself a goddess, the mistress of kingdoms, yet even divinity bends to the will of death. A serpent's kiss, the god's final jest, but my hand writes her true fate: mortal like the rest. Decode the stars she ruled to see my next, a queen among shadows who will pay my debt."

The killer incorporated a star may of key constellations visible in ancient Alexandria, which served as a challenge to investigators like FBI's John Douglas. They needed the meaning behind these clues to determine the next victim based on the position of certain stars. The hidden numerical values seem to correspond to key dates in Cleopatra's life, such as her birth year and death year, encoded to suggest a timeline for the next crime.

Tucked within the letter was a phrase written in Mary MacIntosh's handwriting style, revealing the killer's fixation on her intellect and daring her to solve the cipher before the next murder.

Chapter 6

When John Douglas learned of the cipher for the Cleopatra-staged murder, he called Mac.

"Mac, it's John. I really need your help on this next cipher." He updated her on the scene of the crime and the cipher. Mac's heart sank.

"The killer is obsessed with me," Mac said. "That is not good."

"No, it's not. I called Burg to inform him about it and the need to have surveillance at your home at all times. The FBI is paying for this surveillance and there is a black and white now parked in front of your house. This will remain until we feel like we caught the correct killer," John informed Mac.

"Can you send me the cipher?" Mac asked.

"It's in your inbox now."

"Let me get the boys down for a nap and I will take a look at it and call you back," she promised.

After Mac carefully studied the photos of the murder scene, she noticed that the killer's meticulous staging mirrors not only Cleopatra's death but also the mythological imagery Cleopatra used to bolster her divine image as Isis reincarnated. The ring on the victim's finger resembled that of Cleopatra's signet. The letter's poetic phrasing "Decode the stars she ruled" prompted Mac to look at the celestial theme.

She remembered that Cleopatra was closely associated with the start, particularly Sirius, the "dog star" and the zodiac sign Virgo, tied to Egyptian mythology.

Mac worked on decoding the hieroglyphics using her expertise in ancient languages.   Within the cipher was a numerical reference to Cleopatra's life events, 69, 51, 44, and 30 which depicted her birth year, the year she ascended to the throne, the assassination of Julius Caesar, and her death.

Mac concluded that the sequence suggested a pattern, not just historical but chronological. Using the star map in the hieroglyphs, Mac identified Sirius and Virg as clues. Sirius, linked to rebirth in Egyptian lore, and Virgo, symbolized Cleopatra's divine femininity, pointed to locations or names relevant to the killer's next victim. Mac theorized that "a queen among shadows" referred to a modern figure associated with fame and mystery, possibly a reclusive female celebrity or someone notable for their tragic story.

Mac utilized astronomical software to see when Sirius and Virgo next align, finding a specific date and location where the stars would be prominent in the night sky. Cross-referencing the pattern of dates with famous queens or women from history and mythology could help zero in on symbolic connections.

Mac surmised that the killer's fixation on Cleopatra reflected the killer's view of powerful women as symbolic of their internal rage – women who project their strength but have vulnerabilities the killer exploits.

Mac notes the phrase in her handwriting and sees it as a direct challenge: the killer sees her as a worthy adversary and intellectual equal. This is unnerving to Mac. She called John back.

"Through the cipher and staging, I think we have a narcissistic and highly intelligent individual obsessed with historical figures as a symbol of perceived betrayal. The killer's elaborate recreations of historical deaths hint at a deeper personal connection, likely tied to their childhood fascination with mythology or a fixation on justice against women they feel failed them," Mac explained. "The taunting letters and ciphers echo the Zodiac Killer's MO, but there are subtle differences. This killer is incorporating a theme of divine justice and poetic death."

"That is deep, Mac," John said. Her intelligence never ceased to amaze him.

"I think the killer might see himself or herself as an arbiter of fate, punishing women for imagined slights in a way they view as 'historically justified.' "

"I just got off the phone again with Burg and he is very worried about your safety and the safety of the family. I assured him of the protection and surveillance, but he said that he was going to talk to you tonight about not consulting on the case."

"I need to do this. The killer is taunting me directly. I think that the killer views me as a modern-day Cleopatra – a powerful yet vulnerable woman destined for a tragic end unless I outwit them."

"I don't disagree with your theory," John said.

"By uncovering the historical and symbolic layers in the cipher, I think that the next murder victim will be a target to mimic the death of another famous figure, perhaps Joan of Arc or Marie Antoinette, escalating this killer's motivation to kill. The letters hint that the killer's endgame involves me somehow, not as a victim but as someone they hope will understand their motivations."

Chapter 7

Within a week, another body was found in Miami, and this crime scene was discovered in a secluded battlefield. The scene was shrouded in a thick, eerie fog. Flickering lanterns surrounded the body, mimicking torches. The victim was dressed in a replica of Joan the Arc's armor – a silver breastplate, chainmail coif, and gauntlets – but the material was lightweight and clearly ornamental. She was posed kneeling, hands bound in front as though in prayer, with her head tilted skyward. A crudely crafted wooden cross was placed on her chest.

The body showed signs of burns, but they appeared superficial. The actual cause of the deal is a stab wound to the heart, symbolizing betrayal rather than physical martyrdom. Ash and charred wood were scattered around, arranged in a circular pattern to resemble a medieval stake execution. The killer left a medieval-style banner bearing Joan's coat of arms – a sword flanked by lilies.

Surrounding the scene were scattered pages from a Bible, some burnt at the edges, with specific passages highlighted, likely tied to themes of sacrifice and redemption. The killer left a handwritten letter with a mix of Old French, Latin, and English. The letter taunted investigators to piece together the languages to decode the message.

The letter read: "The Maid of Orleans met her fate, Condemned by those she vowed to save. Her faith burned brighter than flames, but who delivers salvation to the brave? One sword, one lily, one truth concealed, the fire reveals what lies unhealed. Decode her banner to find the next – a crown awaits my final jest."

John once again called Mac to discuss the crime scene and the cipher.

"You will find in your email another file with the details of what we are calling the 'Joan of Arc' murder," John said to Mac.

"Good Lord, another murder?" Mac exclaimed. "That is three in three weeks! This serial killer is prolific!."

"Yes, very. And with such elaborate crime scenes, this murderer is spending a lot of time premeditating the scenes," John said. "People in Miami are freaked out."

"I bet," Mac said. "I'll take a look at the file. Burg's mom is here today to watch the kids and I therefore have time."

Mac opened the file and started to read. Once she was done reviewing the evidence, she called John.

"The mix of languages reflects Joan's ability to bridge different cultures and emphasizes the killer's intellectual challenge to investigators. The Old French portion gives the name of Joan's birthplace, Domremy, which might hint at a specific geographical clue.

Latin passages refer to Biblical texts Joan would have invoked, such as Psalm 23 or Isaiah 54.17, which pointed to a theme of; No weapon formed against you shall power have', which might correspond to numbers in the cipher," Mac said.

"Go on," John begged.

"The killer's use of Joan's coat of arms includes symbols such as a sword, and a lily, which could hold numerical significance when translated into heraldic code. For example, lilies could represent purity and the number three, tied to the Holy Trinity."

"Yes. What about the singed Bible pages?" John asked.

"I think the charred Bible pages could represent the killer's next locations, as the highlighted verses refer to Joan's coronation of Charles VII. This could symbolize royalty, suggesting a site associated with kings or modern monarchies," Mac suggested.

"That's highly possible," John added. "We are noting the killer's fixation on Joan's betrayal by her own people. We think that the killer sees himself as both the betrayed and the betrayer, projecting their inner turmoil onto their victims."

"Oooh, I like that. The reference to 'one sword, one lily, one truth concealed' led me to research Joan's trial and subsequent rehabilitation, hinting that the killer may see himself as unjustly condemned but also as an arbiter of justice.

The phrase 'a crown awaits my final jest' suggests the killer's next victim may be linked to the royalty of power. I see a connection to a modern political figure whose life echoes betrayal or public disgrace," Mac said.

"Our profiler team thinks that the staging could only depict the killer's obsession with female figures who are symbols of power, purity, or martyrdom. Their acts are not just murders but performative reenactments meant to assert their control over history," John said.

"Why do you think the killer is obsessed with me? Burg is highly agitated with me for getting involved in these Midnight Scribe murders."

"We think that the killer's obsession with you grows clearer through his letters and the themes. He sees you as both a Joan of Arc figure fighting for justice and as someone whose conviction he wishes to test. We think he wants to play you into his 'final jest'."

Chapter 8

It wasn't three more days when John called Mac again.

"You were right with respect to the next murder resembling royalty. This murder scene involves the Midnight Scribe's reenacting Marie Antoniett's demise as he staged her murder similarly, which we think that the clues left behind offer rich symbolism tied to opulence, excess, betrayal, and execution." John said.

"Send me the file," Mac said.

"Already in your inbox. But I'll give you the Cliff Note summary. The murder took place in an extravagant setting which is a modern mansion's great ballroom which would have inspired a banquet hall, evoking the decadence of Versailles."

Mac walked over to her laptop and clicked on her inbox. She was perusing the file as John continued his summation.

The room was domed with chandeliers, gilded mirrors, and elaborate candelabras, creating a stark contrast between its beauty and the grisly crime scene. Classical music was playing on an antique phonograph, stuck in an eerie loop of an unfinish the victim was dressed in 18th-century French court attire including a powdered wig, an ornate pastel gown with gold embroidery, and an array of pearls and jewels.

She was positioned as though kneeling before an invisible executioner, her head resting on a replica of a guillotine scaffold. However, the guillotine is only symbolic, the actual cause of death is a deep gash across the throat, meticulously crafted to mimic the clean cut of a blade. Around the victim, scattered props evoke Marie's legacy: a shattered porcelain tea set, an overturned cake stand, and a bloodstained fan.

A severed mannequin head, made to resemble Marie Antoinette, was placed on a silver platter beside the body, which is a chilling nod to the guillotine. A final theatrical tough was a towering cake, left untouched but inscribed with the words, 'Let them eat cake' in red icing."

"That is intense, Mac said. Tell me about the handwritten letter of cipher," Mac asked.

"The handwritten letter, written in elaborate calligraphy on cream-colored parchment, was left of the cake stand. The killer used French phrases and references to the French Revolution to weave a taunting message. It reads, 'Her crown was heavy, her people enraged. A queen betrayed, her head encaged. The blade fell swiftly, and the people cheered, But who bears guilt when all is smeared? In the palace where power is lent, Search for the lily, now torn and bent. For she is my next, her fate already spent.'"

The Midnight Scribe is making elaborate crime scenes. It seems as if it is escalating.

From what I am looking at, he has gone to great lengths to recreate historical details. I see a wooden plank inscribed with 'Liberte, Egalite, Fraternite' near the victim, but the calligraphy seems wrong. This isn't French, it is Latin. On the guillotine's blade was a note taped, written in looping, delicate cursive. After the poem was coded: L B:4, L:13, Z:1, M:7, the Alpha Greek symbol, a crescent moon XII: XIII, 1789, and the symbol of the cross."

Mac zoomed in on the code recognizing the Roman numeral reference to 12:08, likely a time. "John, the crescent moon could be a reference to nighttime or a celestial symbol. The year 1789 could be tied to the French Revolution which was an obvious nod to the victim's Marie Antoniette persona," Mac said.

"What about the other symbols?" John asked her. The omega and the cross hinted at endings and life after death. Are they literal clues or symbolic taunts?"

"This isn't about Marie Antoniette. This is just another piece in a game the killer wants me to play," Mac noted. "And deciphering this cipher to solve these murders must happen swiftly."

Chapter 9

As The Midnight Scribe continued his string of murders, the media was captivated by his theatrical style. Every new cipher was a headline, and armchair detectives, conspiracy theorists, and would-be copycats flooded online forums, attempting to decode the ciphers and predict the killer's next move.

A disturbing fan base emerged online, obsessed with The Midnight Scribe. Some of these individuals were attracted to his commitment to the crime scene and noted his killer's mannerisms in eerie detail.

"John, this media frenzy concerns me, as the hype around this serial killer might be feeding his ego and encouraging him to kill again soon, with another detailed and bizarre crime scene. We are nowhere close to deciphering the Marie Antoinette cipher and it seems like the media attention is fueling the killer's need for recognition and fame," Mac said on the phone to John. "There are folks out there that are highly active on forums, dedicated to analyzing The Midnight Scribe's ciphers. There are multiple usernames expressing admiration for the killer, discussing plans to start 'their own masterpieces' and it has become evident that these echo chambers were fueling dangerous delusions of fame and validation among others."

At the FBI, we are equally concerned about this and we worry that copycat killers will pop up all over the country," John said.

"That concept has crossed my mind. I was lamenting about it last night during dinner with Burg," Mac said.

Chapter 10

The Midnight Scribe's obsession with history's great figures next leads to Ernest Hemingway, a larger-than-life literary icon. Hemingway's themes of isolation, masculinity, and existential struggle resonate with the killer, who seeks to create a tableau that reflects Hemingway's tragic end by his suicide by shotgun at his home in Ketchum, Idaho.

Ernest Hemingway (1899-1961) was an American novelist, short-story writer, and journalist known for his spare prose and adventurous life. He penned classics such as The Old Man and the Sea, For Whom the Bell Tolls, A Farewell to Arms, and The Sun Also Rises. Hemingway won the Pulitzer Prize in 1953 and the Nobel Prize in Literature in 1954.

Hemingway's "iceberg theory" emphasized subtext over exposition, presenting deeper emotions beneath simple, direct language. His works often explored themes of courage, death, love, and disillusionment.

Hemingway's health and mental state deteriorated in his later years, culminating in his suicide in 1961. His struggle with depression, paranoia, and the pressure of maintaining his image influenced the tragic nature of his demise.

The Midnight Scribe staged the crime in a library belonging to a renowned Hemingway collector in Key West, Floria – a nod to Hemingway's time living there.

The setting was the body of a middle-aged man sitting in a leather armchair in the center of the library, surrounded by walls lined with Hemingway's first editions and artifacts. On the coffee table, there was an open typewriter with a blood-spattered page inserted into the roller. The typed message read: "The sun also sets."

The victim was posed in the armchair, wearing a tweed hunting jacket, and holding a replica shotgun. A wide-brimmed hat rested on his knee, and a glass of absinthe sat on the table beside him. The victim's death mirrored Hemingway's suicide; a shotgun blast to the head, though the killer ensured minimal disfigurement to maintain the tableau's aesthetic.

On a nearby bookshelf, the killer left another letter addressed to Mac, written on vintage paper. The letter read, "Dearest Mary, A great man once wrote: 'The world breaks everyone, and afterward, some are strong at the broken places.' But what about those who never recover? What about the ones who shatter entirely? I've given Hemingway his final chapter, though I doubt he would approve of my edits. But it's not about his story, Mary, it's about yours. Do you see the parallel yet? The sun is setting, and soon, you'll have no choice but to meet me at dawn. Decipher this, and you may yet save the next.

The Midnight Scribe. Beneath the letter was another cipher: K:22, H:9, a delta sign, a sunrise, XIII:VII, 1954, and the Leo symbol.

Mac analyzed the cipher with John, and she felt like the K:22 and H:9 might refer to positions in the alphabet or coordinates in a book. The delta symbolizes change or difference, which could suggest a literary twist. The sun was likely a Hemingway reference but could also indicate the time of day. XIII: VII (13:7) could be a time or date, while 1954 alludes to Hemingway's Nobel Prize year. The Leo symbol might point to Hemingway's birth month, July, or someone connected to the case.

"This is more than an homage," Mac said to John. "He's weaving Hemingway's despair into his own narrative, and dragging me along for the ride."

"I agree with your analysis, Mac. We will get to the bottom of this, I promise."

Chapter 11

The FBI's Behavioral Analysis Unit (BAU), with Mac as a consultant, was diving deeper into profiling The Midnight Scribe. By analyzing the killer's fixation on famous figures, the theatrical crime scenes, and the personalized letters to Mac, the team agreed that the killer's mix of intellect, narcissism, and meticulous planning suggested a highly intelligent and egotistical individual who craves recognition.

The team focused on the killer's apparent obsession with history, literature, and symbolism. The BAU considered whether the killer had a background in academia, journalism, or the arts.

Drawing from her legal and investigative experience, Mac provided insight into the Scribe's taunting letters. She argued that the killer's obsession with her was personal, suggesting they may have studied her career or even crossed paths with her before.

The FBI Evidence Response Team (ERT) was meticulously processing the Hemingway scene. They were collecting trace evidence from fibers, DNA, fingerprints, etc., from the stated victim, the shotgun, and the library. They were in the process of reviewing security footage of nearby cameras for suspicious activity.

The forensic linguistics at the FBI were examining the killer's letters for unique writing quirks, ink or paper analysis, and word choice to pinpoint their identity or geographic origin.

They were busy comparing the handwriting to previous letters.

Given the high-profile nature of the case, the FBI was coordinating with media teams to handle public relations. By choosing to withhold specific details about the staged scenes and ciphers to prevent copycats or leaks that could interfere with the investigation. Announcements were made to the public to follow safety guidelines, particularly for individuals in literary, artistic, or historical circles who might fit the Scribe's target profile.

Investigators were examining connections between the victims. Hemingway and Marie Antoniette were analyzed in tandem. Were they members of the same social circles? Did they share any public affiliations, such as books, historical societies, or literary events?

Were the victims symbolic stand-ins for historical figures, or were they specifically targeted for personal reasons? Could their personalities or achievements have provoked envy or resentment in the killer?

Using the cipher as a guide, the FBI would anticipate the next target. They were combining elements from the cipher such as locations, and historical dates, with the killer's established themes to narrow down potential targets. The FBI was reaching out to experts in history, history, literature, and art to gather insight into the killer's inspirations and possible future choices.

Believing the Midnight Scribe would attempt another high-profile murder, the FBI employed countermeasures. Surveillance was being put in motion, placing known historians, writers, and figures who embody historical archetypes under protective watch. They were planning to use an undercover agent to pose as a potential target, hoping to lure the killer into revealing himself.

While the FBI was focused on traditional methods, Mac was following a more intuitive, unconventional approach. She was examining her own life for links to the killer. Did the killer choose her as a correspondent because of a specific case she prosecuted or a publicized trial? She had immersed herself in Hemingway's works and the histories of other famous figures to uncover hidden clues. She pondered her connection to Hemingway in that he wrote A Farewell to Arms in Sheridan, Wyoming, while staying at The Historic Sheridan Inn. Could the prosecution of both the Red Hands Killer and the Dating Game Killer have a role in that she prosecuted both highly publicized cases?

Mac was not sure. But she knew that she was racing against time to answer these questions.

Chapter 12

Vincent van Gogh (1853-1890) is one of history's most celebrated painters, known for his emotional intensity and innovative use of color. Despite his posthumous fame, his life was marked by poverty, mental illness, and personal tragedy. Van Gogh produced over 2,1000 artworks, including approximately 860 oil paintings, many of which are now considered masterpieces.

Born in the Netherlands, he initially worked as an art dealer and preacher before committing to painting in his early twenties. His artistic career lasted just a decade. His work is known for its vibrant colors, bold brushstrokes, and emotive energy. Famous works include Starry Night, Sunflowers, The Bedroom, and The Café Terrace at Night.

Van Gogh struggled with severe mental illness, experiencing psychotic episodes and depression. He famously cut off part of his ear in 1888, followed by a conflict with fellow artist Paul Gauguin.

In 1890, Van Gogh died at the age of 37, likely from a self-inflicted gunshot wound. However, some theories suggest that he may have been accidentally shot by local boys.

During his lifetime, Van Gogh sold only one painting. Today his work is celebrated globally, symbolizing the misunderstood genius and the fine line between brilliance and madness.

The Midnight Scribe, inspired by Van Gogh's tragic life and misunderstood genius, staged a haunting recreation of his death – but with the artistic flair of his iconic works.

The murder was staged in an art gallery that resembled the one in Arles, France, where Van Gogh lived and painted some of his most famous works. The art gallery was transformed into a surreal homage to Van Gogh's most famous painting. A Starry Night backdrop covered the walls, with twinkling lights resembling the stars. Replicas of Van Gogh's Sunflowers were scattered on the floor, their stems broken and petals smeared with blood. In the center of the room, the victim was posed in a wooden chair, mimicking Van Gogh's The Bedroom.

The victim, an artist known for their Van Gogh-inspired work, was dressed in a tattered blue smock, with a palette and brush placed in their hands. Their left ear had been severed and placed in a jar labeled "For Mary."

The victim was shot in the chest, but the bullet wound was artfully concealed by sunflowers pinned to his clothing. The Midnight Scribe left a letter pinned to the chair, written in jagged, erratic handwriting that resembled brushstrokes.

It read, "Dearest Mary, Genius often walks hand in hand with despair. Vincent understood this trust, and now my artist does too. Their masterpiece is complete, but yours is still unfinished. Can you see the pattern emerging? Each scene is a painting, a story, a cry for understanding. Follow the colors, the brushstrokes, the stars. Decode the light, and perhaps you can find the next canvas before it's painted in blood. With admiration and expectation, The Midnight Scribe."

Beneath the lettering was another cipher: V:7, G9, a pair of scissors, a crescent moon, XIX:VII, 1888, and a star. Upon assembling the file to email to Mac, he called her.

"It's John. I just sent you an email with the most recent Midnight Scribe killing in the art studio in Miami After you have had an opportunity to review the case, call me back to discuss," John said to Mac.

"Good timing, Mac said. The kiddos are napping and I was working on prepping dinner. I'll take a look now," Mac said.

As she previewed the file, the severed ear and use of Van Gogh's iconography suggested the killer's fascination with pain, genius, and legacy. Mac called John.

"The use of specific dates like 1888 when Van Gogh cut off his ear hinted at a timeline for the next murder. The cipher obviously holds clues about the next target, perhaps another misunderstood artist or a location tied to Van Gogh," Mac said.

"Our profilers are analyzing the gallery for traces of the killer's DNA or fingerprints. The jar containing the ear is being examined for forensic evidence and symbolic meaning," John said.

"I think that the killer sees himself as a tortured genius like Van Gogh, someone who feels misunderstood by the world," Mac offered.

As Mac worked on deciphering the letter and the killer's intentions, she realized the next victim might be a living artist or public figure who embodied the struggle between creativity and madness. The challenge would be to anticipate which artist or location the Scribe would target next, based on Van Gogh's legacy.

"This isn't just about murder," Mac said. "The Scribe is creating their own tragic masterpiece, and he wants me to be its curator. But to the killer, I'm also a blank canvas – someone they can shape into their ultimate creation. We need to stop them before the next stroke of their brush becomes another life lost. We need to race against time, knowing the Midnight Scribe's next tableau would be even more haunting and symbolic."

"Agreed," John said. The FBI profiling and forensic team is working around the clock on this one. We know what is at stake."

Chapter 13

The problem they were facing was the media frenzy. Every new cipher made the national headlines, and the obsession with the Midnight Scribe was growing epic. His disturbing fan base continued to grow online and these fans were attracted to the killer's commitment to elaborate crime scenes.

Millions of fans who obsessed with the Midnight Scribe followed each other on social media. Someone had established an Instagram account entitled The Midnight Scribe and it had over a million followers. Someone else had created a YouTube channel with the same name, and the channel had over two million subscribers. There was even a Facebook page dedicated to the killer, with thousands of comments and theories.

Mac knew that the case had wheels and that they could not slow the media frenzy, and this put tremendous pressure on law enforcement to get ahead of this. They had no suspects. Not one shred of evidence pointed in the direction of a suspect. This was a tremendous problem.

Chapter 14

Burg was growing ever so leery of his wife's involvement in this case. He knew that it was dangerous for her to be involved, and he resented her for not putting their family first. Having 24-hour surveillance at their home did not calm Burg. In fact, it caused the opposite, as it was an hourly reminder that the family was at risk.

Mac wanted to go to Miami to work with John, but Burg put his foot down on that idea. First of all, they had four babies under the age of two, and they needed their mother at home to take care of them. Also, Burg felt like she was able to participate just fine with email, telephone calls and Zoom. She did not need to be at the scene of a crime, as this would clearly put her life in danger. Burg talked to John about it, and even John agreed that Mac was not safe at the scene of these gruesome crimes.

Mac was a strong, professional woman, and she didn't like being told what to do and Burg was well aware of her stubbornness. But he was not conceding on this one.

He felt the cold shoulder in the bedroom, and she waited until he was asleep to slip into bed. She was gone before he awoke, and the silence in the household between them was cutting.

Luckily, the home was rife with joy and noise due to the kids, but their marriage was strained and they both knew it.

Chapter 15

Media attention was driving more murders. New segments and talk shows debated the ethics of covering The Midnight Scribe so extensively. Mac and John are torn by this, knowing that information is power and that the more educated people are about this dangerous killer, the more likely they will exercise caution. John admitted that the media sensation resembled that of the Zodiac Killer and that it was both positive and negative.

They could not stop the train of the media. This was the biggest news story in the country, and it was the media's job to report it. Mac and John understood this. But they were also concerned about the sensational message of the crimes and worried that this might inspire copycat murders.

Chapter 16

Albert Einstein (1879-1955) was a theoretical physicist whose groundbreaking work transformed our understanding of the universe. Known as the father of modern physics, he developed the theory of relativity and contributed to quantum mechanics, thermodynamics, and cosmology. Einstein's intellectual genius and moral philosophy have made him an enduring symbol of human potential and curiosity.

Born in Germany, Einstein showed an early curiosity for mathematics and science but struggled with formal schooling due to his rigid structure. He earned a doctorate in physics in 1905, a year often referred to as his Annus Mirabilis (miracle year) for producing four groundbreaking papers.

He introduced the Theory of Relativity and the famous equation E = mc2, showing the relationship between energy and mass. His Quantum Theory of Light proposed that light behaves as both a wave and particle, foundational to quantum mechanics. His work laid the groundwork for the development of atomic energy, though he opposed its use in warfare.

Einstein was a pacifist, humanitarian, and advocate for civil rights. His later years were dedicated to unifying physics' fundamental forces, though he never completed this "theory of everything."

He died in 1955 of an aortic aneurysm. He famously refused surgery, saying, "I want to go when I want to go. It is tasteless to prolong life artificially."

His brain was removed for study without his consent, an ironic twist for a man whose intellectual brilliance defined him.

The Midnight Scribe turned Einstein's legacy into a grotesque yet symbolic crime scene, using the physicist's work and philosophy as inspiration for their macabre tableau.

The murder took place in Princeton, New Jersey, where Einstein spent his later years teaching at the Institute for Advanced Study. The scene was staged in an abandoned observatory. The observatory was transformed into a warped representation of Einstein's most famous concepts: A large chalkboard dominated the room, filled with equations, including the ominous inclusion of $E = mc2$, rewritten as $E = m*d2$ meaning energy means mines times death squared. A broken clock was hanging from the ceiling, its hands stopped at 3:55, the time of Einstein's death. Around the room, shattered mirrors reflected distorted images, symbolizing the relativity of perception.

The victim was a renowned physicist known for championing Einstein's work. He was positioned at a desk as if mid-calculation, with his head resting on a notebook filled with equations. His brain had been surgically removed and placed in a glass jar labeled "Relic of Genius."

A stopwatch was clutched in his hand, frozen at exactly one minute before midnight – a node to the Midnight Scribe's name.

The victim was poisoned, possibly symbolizing Einstein's belief in natural death and the rejection of artificial prolongation of life.

The Midnight Scribe left another chilling letter addressed to Mary MacIntosh, written on vintage parchment in a precise, scientific font. The letter read: "To My Eternal Student, Mary MacIntosh, What is time but a construct? What is life but energy waiting to be transformed? Einstein understood the dance between creation and destruction, between chaos and order. Now, so do I. This is my Theory of Relativity: The closer you are to me, the faster lives unravel. The further you are, the slower justice crawls. But justice is meaningless if the equation is incomplete. Solve this, and you may find your way to my Event Horizon. Ignore it, and the next genius will fall. Time is an illusion, Mary. But death? Death is an absolute truth. The Midnight Scribe."

Below the letter was a cipher scrawled on the chalkboard: E:1, infinity sign, h (Planck's constant), A:3:55, Princeton, 1905, a Pisces sign.

The minute that John was informed of the crime, he called Mac.

Chapter 17

The FBI was overwhelmed by evidence from The Midnight Scribe killings. The team could not keep up. There was a lot of pressure on John and his team to find a scrap of evidence for this serial killer, but thus far, they had not one piece of DNA or any circumstantial evidence to link these murders to a suspect.

Investigators were focusing on the removal of the brain, looking for surgical precision or tools that could link the killer to a specific background, such as medicine or neuroscience.

The poison was being analyzed to identify its source, potentially leading to the killer's location or educational background.

The focus on Einstein's brain suggested that the Scribe was fixated on the intersection of intellect and mortality. The precise staging indicated that the killer had scientific knowledge, possibly someone with access to academic circles or research institutions.

The team was working to decode the scientific symbols and references in the cipher, possibly hinting at the next target, time, or location.

The h, Planck's constant, could signify a connection to quantum mechanics. 1905 points to Einstein's Miracle Year – perhaps an anniversary or reference to a nearby event. The Pisces sign could hint at a person or location with astrological ties.

Once the evidence was gathered and the investigation was underfoot, John called Mac.

"We have another one," John said to Mac.

"I saw it on the news," Mac replied.

"I've just completed the FBI forensic file and have emailed it to you."

"Yes, I saw it come through. I need to finish feeding the babies breakfast and it will be a few hours of kiddo play time, but when I get them down for their naps, I will look at the file and call you back."

"You are the best, Mac."

"We need to solve this, John. He is getting richer in character and the media is eating this up, and I am desperately worried about his fan base."

"Me too. Talk to you soon."

The phone went dead.

Chapter 18

Mac opened the file and took a deep delve into Einstein's life and work, seeking deeper meaning behind the Scribe's symbolism. In her mind, she thought that the killer was trying to reconcile his own feelings of intellectual inadequacy by "reclaiming" the genius of history's great minds.

Once she reviewed the entire file, she called John.

"This isn't just about murder – it's about obsession. The Scribe sees himself as part of a higher intellectual game, one where life and death are pawns in his twisted pursuit of meaning. Einstein believed in unifying the universe's forces. The Scribe believes in unifying his victims into one grand equation – and I'm the constant in his formula," Mac suggested.

"We are facing mounting pressure from the public and the top guns as The Midnight Scribe's intellectual prowess and meticulous planning have pushed us to our limits. The cipher and Einstein's legacy are a hint at a larger, more horrifying pattern yet to be uncovered," John said.

"No question. The intensity of the crimes and the frequency have me grossly worried, but the media frenzy, fan base, and social media interactions from this fan base are what elevate this to a higher place. Have you been paying attention to Instagram, YouTube and Facebook

"The Midnight Scribe" pages? They are outsourcing more fans than A-list celebrities and rock bands. That is of grave concern," Mac said.

"Yes. It is a terminal situation, and we have absolutely no evidence of suspects. My boss is beyond herself."

"She should be.

Chapter 19

Mac and Burg were not getting along better and it had been weeks since they had communicated about anything other than their kids and schedules. The tension could be cut with a knife in their household. And just when she thought it could not get worse, it did.

When Burg got home from work that day, he grabbed the mail from the mailbox on their front lawn and was rifling through it as he walked in the door. It was stopped cold in his tracks. There was a letter in his hands addressed to his wife and the mother of his children and the return sender only had three words. "The Midnight Scribe."

Burg walked into the kitchen to find Mac feeding the four children dinner. Her hair was a mess and she had bags under her eyes with smeared mascara and was in her sweats that were dirty and torn and one of his T-shirts. He felt sorry for her but was also pissed at her. His heart was torn.

"Here you go. I hope this makes you happy," Burg said to Mac as he shoved the letter her way in an aggressive manner.

Mac looked at the envelope and her eyes grew wide. She looked up at her husband and started to cry.

Chapter 20

Burg assumed baby duties and relieved Mac while she went downstairs to her office in private to read the letter from The Midnight Scribe.

"Dearest Mary, I saved my most beautiful tragedy for last. Marilyn was adored by millions but understood by none. She was a dream, a muse, and an illusion – a perfect reflection of what you are to me. Fame is fleeting, Mary, but the legacy is eternal. I've left mine in the lines of these letters, the brushstrokes of my murders. You are my audience, my critic, and my inspiration. And now, my masterpiece is complete. The spotlight fades, the curtain falls, and all that remains is applause – or silence. Forever yours, The Midnight Scribe."

Under the signature line was the cipher: M:62, C:7, a star, a broken heart, MM:6:19, an envelope, Hollywood, JFK.

Mac quickly scanned and emailed the letter to John before calling him.

"Check your inbox. The Midnight Scribe sent what he refers to as his final cipher to my home address," Mac said on the phone to John.

"What?"

"I'm not joking. Open the attachment and look at it. I'll wait. Burg got the mail and I put myself into time out because he is fuming."

"I can't say that I blame him, Mac. I'm grateful for your help, but it has placed you and your family at risk. The fact that the Scribe knows your home address is terrifying."

"I know."

"Go unite with your family and I will share this with the team."

"I will. Thanks."

Chapter 21

Marilyn Monroe (1926-1962) was one of Hollywood's most iconic stars, known for her beauty, charm, and vulnerability. Despite her glamorous persona, Monroe's life was fraught with personal struggles, making her a tragic figure in popular culture. Her mysterious death continues to captivate the public and fuel conspiracy theories.

Born Norma Jeane Mortenson, Monroe overcame a troubled childhood in foster homes and orphanages. She rose to stardom in the 1950s with films like *Gentlemen Prefer Blondes*, *Some Like it Hot*, and *The Seven Year Itch*.

Known for her "blonde bombshell" image, Monroe became a symbol of femininity, desire, and Hollywood glamour. Behind the scenes, she was intelligent, deeply insecure, and often exploited by the industry.

Monroe struggled with depression, addiction, and failed relationships, including marriages to Joe DiMaggio and Arthur Miller. She had rumored ties to the Kennedys, fueling speculations about her affair with JFK and about her death.

She was found dead in her Los Angeles home in 1962, officially ruled a probable suicide from a barbiturate overdose. Conspiracy theories suggest foul play involving the government, the Mafia, or Hollywood elites.

The Midnight Scribe's final murder is his piece de resistance, staged to symbolize both the fragility of fame and the cost of human vulnerability. It mirrored Monroe's traffic life and enigmatic death, marking the culmination of the killer's "masterpiece."

The murder took place in a luxury hotel suite in Los Angeles, meticulously decorated to resemble Monroe's final home. The room was adorned with 1950s Hollywood glamour: velvet curtains, vintage mirrors, and a red carpet leading to the victim's body. A champagne glass lay overturned on the vanity, alongside a lipstick tube that spelled out "Goodbye, Mary" on the mirror. The bed was covered in white satin sheets, with the victim positioned in a recreation of Monroe's famous pose from *The Seven Year Itch*.

The victim was a Marilyn Monroe lookalike -- young and upcoming actress known for her striking resemblance to the star. She was found lying on the bed, wearing a replica of Monroe's iconic white dress. A prescription bottle with the victim's name sat on the nightstand, filled with identical capsules to those in Monroe's toxicology report.

The victim was poisoned, but the staging implied an overdose. A small needle mark on her wrist suggested the killer used a sedative before the final dose.

The killer's final letter, the copy of which had been sent to Mac, was left on the nightstand, handwritten on a sheet of pink stationery.

After John had assembled the Monroe file, he emailed it to Mac. Mac waited until the two sets of twins were in bed for the night to open the file. Burg was asleep, and she needed her alone time and privacy to digest what was about to unravel.

John's summary was read first. It was his analysis of the crime scene. The prescription pills, needle mark, and lipstick note suggest the killer deliberately recreated Monroe's death but with enough devotion to draw attention to his obsession with Mac. The personalization of the note to Mac indicated the Scribe had been escalating his fixation on her.

The Scribe's use of Monroe as his final victim suggested his obsession with fame, beauty, and the fragility of legacy. John made a sidenote to Mac that she carried fame, beauty and the fragility of motherhood.

The FBI profiling team suggested that they were connecting the lookalike victim to the Scribe, possibly tracing auditions or casting calls that targeted women resembling Monroe.

Decoding the cipher was going to prove tricky. M:62 likely referred to Monroe's death in 1962. MM:6:19 could hint at Monroe's initials or a specific time of day in the final murder. Hollywood, JFK suggested ties to Monroe's rumored affair with John F. Kennedy, perhaps pointing investigators toward political or entertainment circles.

Investigators were examining the needle and prescription bottle for fingerprints or DNA traces. The lipstick could provide insights into the killer's movements, as it might be a custom item or contain identifiable reside.

Mac recognized the deeply personal nature of the Scribe's final act, understanding that this crime was meant as a message to her. The deliberate choice of Monroe – a symbol of misunderstood vulnerability and exploited fame – paralleled the Scribe's fixation on Mac as both muse and adversary.

She waited until morning to call John.

"This wasn't just another murder. It was the killer's swan song, their way of claiming immortality. But his legacy isn't in the victims he chose – it's in the patterns he left behind. And that's how we will find him," Mac said.

Chapter 22

The MacIntosh/Burgess household was quiet except for the rhythmic creak of the porch swing, stirred by the night breeze. Mac sat at the kitchen table, the remains of a lukewarm coffee before her, and her FBI case file spread open like a wound she couldn't stop poking. Burg had taken the four kids to his sister's house for the weekend, a rare gift of solitude for Mac to focus on and for Burg to consider his options. Their marriage was on the rocks due to her obsession with The Midnight Scribe, and Burg did not feel that his kids were safe at home, despite the surveillance black and white parked in front of their home.

The quiet had started to unnerve her, as she was used to at least one baby crying, and her sixth sense was jabbing her. She did not feel like she was truly alone.

Their dog, D.B. Cooper, a yellow lab, growled softly from the living room. This was not unusual, as D.B. growled at the mailman, the UPS driver, and anyone else who breached his boundary of the front yard. He stood and shook, and Mac could hear the small bell on his collar shake. She peeked in as it was late, and D.B.'s hair on the back of his neck was standing on end, and his ears went from flat to perked. Mac's pulse quickened. She reached for Burg's handgun she kept in the rafter of their coat closet. She nearly jumped when she heard a soft knock on the front door, hesitant but deliberate.

Mac opened her phone and opened the Ring door camera to see who could possibly be knocking at 11:30 at night. She thought it was possible that it was one of the police officers noting that a light was on and asking to use the restroom, which happened from time to time. But this was not a face that she recognized. And then, just like that, he was gone. She moved slowly, gripping the gun tight, and peered through the peephole. No one was there.

Then, she saw it. A figure standing on the lawn, illuminated by the porch light – a man in a tailored black suit and a wide-brimmed hat. His face was pale and gaunt, almost skeletal, but his eyes were burning with something Mac couldn't quite name. Recognition hit her like a freight train.

It was him. The Midnight Scribe.

Stupidly, she threw the door open, weapon raised, wondering what happened to the surveillance cop. She could see him in his squad car, slumped over the wheel.

"Stay where you are!" Mac commanded in a loud voice.

He didn't flinch. Slowly, he raised his hands, revealing a folded piece of paper in his left hand. He stepped forward, stopping just at the edge of the porch, and slowly bent over and placed the paper gently on the wooden railing.

"For you," he said, his voice eerily calm. "The final chapter."

"Get on the ground, face down, arms behind your back!" Mac ordered, her voice trembling but steady.

Instead, he smiled. It was a sad, haunting smile, and he reached into his jacket. Mac's finger tightened on the trigger, but before she could react, he pulled out a shotgun.

"Wait!" Mac screamed, lowering her weapon slightly, her mind racing for an angle to de-escalate.

He looked at her with something like reverence, tears streaming down his hollow cheeks. "You gave me meaning, Mary. You made me feel seen. But I'm a monster, and you deserve peace."

"Don't do this!" Mac pleaded, stepping forward.

"I'll always love you," he whispered, his voice breaking. Then, in one fluid motion, he turned the shotgun to his chest and pulled the trigger, Hemingway and Van Gogh style.

The blast shattered the silence of the night. Mac screamed at his body crumpled to the ground, blood pooling beneath him like ink spilled from a pen.

The security guard awoke from the squad car and rushed to her side, calling for backup on his walkie-talkie. He had his hand on his holster, ready to engage his firearm if necessary.

Neighbors' porch lights flicked on, and people in their nightgowns and robes slowly peeked out to see what the commotion was all about. Her next-door neighbor, Jennifer, asked, "Is everything okay?"

"No, Jennifer, it is not. This man just suicide in my yard," Mac replied, still panting from panic.

Law enforcement arrived within minutes, as did a firetruck and an ambulance. A forensic police officer arrived on the scene, and she first photographed the scene before collecting DNA and fingerprints.

Jennifer approached and hugged Mac. "Let's get you inside and settled. I'll make you some tea," she suggested.

"Ms. MacIntosh, the security guard said, I think you should call your husband."

Jennifer grabbed Mac's cell phone and dialed. Burg groggily picked up.

"Burg, it's Jennifer. Something terrible has happened. Mac is okay, but there is a dead man in your yard. She says that it is The Midnight Scribe and that he shot himself with a shotgun after confronting Mac."

Burg, who was on speakerphone, said, "Oh my God, please put her on the phone!"

Jennifer passed the phone to Mac, who was still shaking on the living room couch. "Are you okay?" Burg asked.

"Yes, just shaken. I'm grateful that the kids aren't here," Mac said.

"I'll pack them up tomorrow morning and come home. We need some much overdue family time," Burg said.

"Yes. Please come home to me."

Chapter 23

Later, inside the house, Mac sat on the couch, staring at the blood-streaked letter in her hand. She promised to turn it over to the police after she had a chance to read it. The words were scrawled in his familiar script, jagged and desperate.

"The story ends with me, so yours can continue. Thank you for being my muse, my obsession, my salvation. Goodbye, Mary."

Her hands trembled, and tears blurred the words, but she refused to let them fall. The weight of his fixation pressed down on her chest, but there was also a strange, sickening sense of relief.

The Midnight Scribe was gone.

But as Mac's eyes scanned the room, her gaze landed on her children's photographs on the mantle. Burg's laugh echoed faintly in her mind. She was alive and so was her family.